Shoo, Fly!
You Can't Eat Here

LILLER HAMILTON

Outskirts Press, Inc.
http://www.outskirtspress.com

Paperback ISBN: 978-1-4787-5383-4
Hardback ISBN: 978-1-4787-5384-1

Library of Congress Control Number: 2015907697

Outskirts Press and the "OP" logo are trademarks belonging to Outskirts Press, Inc.

PRINTED IN THE UNITED STATES OF AMERICA

DENVER, COLORADO

This Book Belongs to:

_____

One day as we entered the cafeteria for lunch, a fly flew in also. He must have been very hungry because…

He tried to land on Mary's brown rice. She waved her hand and said, "Shoo, fly, you can't eat here."

He tried to land on Carlo's steamed broccoli. Carlo waved his hand and shouted, "Shoo, fly, you can't eat here!"

He tried to land on Chasity's baked chicken. She waved her hand and with a squeaky voice said, "Shoo, fly, you can't eat here."

He tried to take a sip of Brandon's milk. Brandon waved his hand and yelled, "Shoo, fly, you can't eat here!"

He tried to nibble on Betty's whole wheat bread. She waved her hand and whispered, "Shoo, fly, you can't eat here."

Finally, he tried to taste Leah's mixed fruit. She waved her hand and with a soft voice said, "Shoo, fly, you can't eat here."

By that time all the children were waving their hands and saying, "Shoo, fly, you can't eat here! Shoo, fly, you can't eat here!"

When the next class opened the door to come into the cafeteria, the hungry fly flew outside to find lunch somewhere else.

The End

CPSIA information can be obtained at www.ICGtesting.com
Printed in the USA
BVIW12n1321040815
411774BV00001B/1

(